Dear Parent:
Your child's love of reading starts here!

Every child learns to read in a different way and at his or her own speed. Some go back and forth between reading levels and read favorite books again and again. Others read through each level in order. You can help your young reader improve and become more confident by encouraging his or her own interests and abilities. From books your child reads with you to the first books he or she reads alone, there are I Can Read Books for every stage of reading:

SHARED READING
Basic language, word repetition, and whimsical illustrations, ideal for sharing with your emergent reader

BEGINNING READING
Short sentences, familiar words, and simple concepts for children eager to read on their own

READING WITH HELP
Engaging stories, longer sentences, and language play for developing readers

READING ALONE
Complex plots, challenging vocabulary, and high-interest topics for the independent reader

ADVANCED READING
Short paragraphs, chapters, and exciting themes for the perfect bridge to chapter books

I Can Read Books have introduced children to the joy of reading since 1957. Featuring award-winning authors and illustrators and a fabulous cast of beloved characters, I Can Read Books set the standard for beginning readers.

A lifetime of discovery begins with the magical words **"I Can Read!"**

Visit www.icanread.com for information on enriching your child's reading experience.

Fancy Nancy: Mademoiselle Mom
Copyright © 2019 by Disney Enterprises, Inc.
All rights reserved. Printed in the United States of America.
No part of this book may be used or reproduced in any manner whatsoever without written permission except
in the case of brief quotations embodied in critical articles and reviews. For information address HarperCollins
Children's Books, a division of HarperCollins Publishers, 195 Broadway, New York, NY 10007.
www.icanread.com

ISBN 978-0-06-288867-9 (trade bdg.) —ISBN 978-0-06-284383-8 (pbk.)

Book design by Brenda E. Angelilli and Scott Petrower

19 20 21 22 23   LSCC   10 9 8 7 6 5 4 3 2 1

First Edition

I Can Read!

BEGINNING 1 READING

DISNEY Junior

Fancy NANCY

Mademoiselle Mom

Adapted by Nancy Parent
Based on the episode
by Sarah Katin and
Nakia Trower Shuman

Illustrations by the
Disney Storybook
Art Team

HARPER
An Imprint of HarperCollinsPublishers

Sacrebleu! Oh no!

Mom has a terrible cold.

"Achoo!" she sneezes.

Then she blows her nose.

JoJo doesn't notice that

Mom is sick.

She just wants to play.

"Those sniffles sound awful," I say.
"You need to go to your room
and rest, *mademoiselle*!"
That's French for young lady.

"That's sweet, Nancy," Mom says,
"but there's too much to do."

"I can help," I tell Mom.

"I can watch JoJo."

"I'm practically an expert
at being a big sister," I tell her.
"I could use a nap," says Mom.

"Don't worry," I say.

"I have everything under control."

"Okay, Nancy," says Mom.

"You're in charge."

"I'm Mom for the day," I say.

I imagine what that will be like.

Everything will be *parfait*!

That's French for perfect!

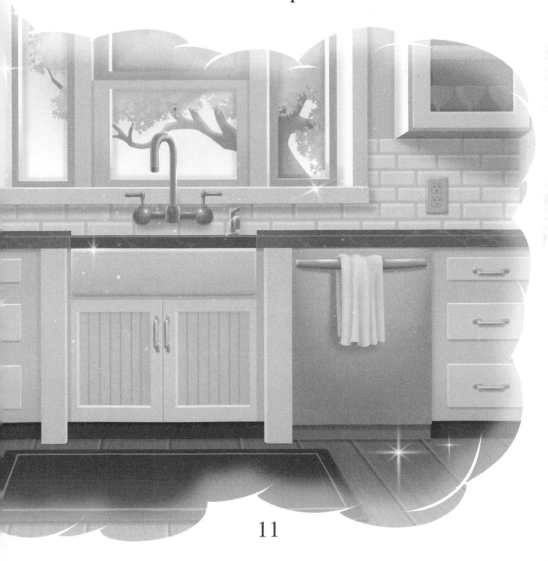

Suddenly JoJo tugs on my skirt.

"I'm hungry," she says.

"I want PB and J."

I look around.

The kitchen is messy.

The towels need folding.

But JoJo's snack comes first.

JoJo takes a juice box.

"Put the straw in," she says.

"Say 'please,'" I tell her

in my best Mom voice.

The straw goes in.

A big squirt comes out!

"Oops, sorry," says JoJo.

"I miss Mommy!" JoJo says.

She runs to the stairs.

But I stop her just in time.

"If you wake Mommy,
we can't play my fun game," I say.
"It's called folding towels!"

But JoJo wants to play pirate.

She hops into the basket.

I grab all the clean towels.

"Whoa!" says JoJo. "A wave!"

"Are you going to eat
your snack, JoJo?" I ask.
I go to wrap it up for later.
But Frenchy gets there first!

Then it gets very quiet.

I see JoJo trying to sneak upstairs.

"Wait!" I say. "Mom's resting."

"But I want Mommy!"

she says.

"I'll play pirate with you," I say.

JoJo smiles.

"I'm the captain!" she says.

How does Mom do it all?

I know! She always does more

than one thing at a time.

I try it!

First I spin JoJo.

Then I fold the towels.

Then I wipe the counter.

Next I load the dishwasher.

"The more soap," I say,

"the cleaner the dishes will be."

Bubbles come pouring

out of the dishwasher!

This is more than bad.

It is terrible!

"I need Mom!" I say.

I run upstairs.

Mom is asleep.

Since I'm in charge,

I guess it's up to *moi*!

That's French for me.

I go back to the kitchen.

JoJo and Frenchy are

playing in the bubbles.

I use towels to mop up the mess.

Then Dad comes home.

"Mom left me in charge," I say.

"Maybe I should help," he says.

"Thanks," I say. "If you insist."

When Mom comes downstairs,
the kitchen sparkles.
"It looks like the whole room
took a bath," she says.

I am pooped!

I think I'll let Mom

be in charge again.

And I'll go back to being *moi*!

Fancy Nancy's Fancy Words

These are the fancy words in this book:

Sacrebleu—French for oh no

Mademoiselle—French for young lady

Parfait—French for perfect

Terrible—more than bad

Moi—French for me